# MILLY HOWARD

# ON YONDER MOUNTAIN

**for grade one**

Designed for use with *READING for Christian Schools*® *1* and
for the reading enjoyment of children of comparable ages

Bob Jones University Press, Greenville, South Carolina 29614

Lesson plans for teaching this book are included in
READING for Christian Schools® 1-2: Teacher's Manual.

**On Yonder Mountain**

Edited by Rebecca Moore

Cover and illustations by Stephanie True

©1989 by Bob Jones University Press
Greenville, South Carolina 29614

ISBN 0-89084-462-3
Printed in the United States of America

20   19   18   17   16   15   14   13

To Evanna Walker,
a most lively teacher

# Publisher's Note

Sarah's story grew from a collection of stories written by Gail Yost about Joy Heath's great-grandmother. These stories, included in the first edition of the Bob Jones University Press first-grade English materials, were intended to teach spiritual lessons that are applicable to today's students. Although the novel has a historical setting, children will relate to the difficulties that Sarah must face.

Sarah is neither a difficult, troubled child nor a child with adult understanding of spiritual matters. She is simply a child, like any other child. She is loving but impatient, lively but sensitive. Sarah's way of dealing with the problems that arise during her first year at school provides positive spiritual teaching for readers of any age.

# Contents

# Chapter One
# The Only Girl

Sarah was as wiggly as a worm inching across a sandy road. She sat her floppy rag doll upright for the third time. She smoothed the front of her new pinafore. Then she swung around to look for her older brother who had gone out to hitch up old Clancy.

"Sarah Goodwin, don't fidget so," her mother said. "School won't start without you. Finish your breakfast."

Sarah fiddled with the pancakes on her plate. She pushed them this way and that way. She couldn't eat one bite.

When Father raised his eyebrows, Ma smiled. "First day jitters," she said quietly.

"My Sarah?" Father's big, booming laugh made Sarah jump. "Jitters? Why, she'll be reading circles around everybody else by noontime."

Sarah giggled. The fluttery feeling in her stomach eased a little. After all, she had learned her alphabet from the boys. And she could read a few words. If the boys could do it, so could she.

"May I go now, Ma?" she asked eagerly. "May I?"

"All right, Sarah," Mother said, smiling. "Come here."

Sarah grabbed EmmyLou from the chair. She stuffed the doll into the deep pocket of her pinafore and went to her mother.

Ma tied and retied the sash on Sarah's pinafore. Sarah did her best to stand still. While her mother smoothed Sarah's long brown braids, she just wiggled her toes in her new shoes. At last the new shiny lunch pail was in her hands, and a kiss was planted on her cheek.

"Come on, Sarah," Thomas called from the yard. "Old Clancy is doing his best to trim Ma's daisy patch!"

Sarah bolted out of the house to join her brothers.

They had already straddled the big horse's back. Sarah clutched her new pail and jumped. In a flurry of tangled skirts, she landed behind William. She turned back to wave as the old horse plodded out of the yard.

"Sarah Elizabeth," her mother scolded, throwing up her hands. "Don't you climb on Old Clancy like that at school! Remember, you're a girl, not a boy!"

Sarah's braids swung as she looked back. "Okay, Ma. I promise!"

"Have a good day!"

"We will, Ma," Sarah called, waving happily.

Clancy's shambling walk jolted Sarah back and forth on his bony spine. She scooted closer to William. William had the best place. His thin legs were stretched across the widest part of Clancy's back. Sarah leaned past his arm to see the road that wound down the mountain.

"Don't strangle me," William protested.

Sarah settled back with a sigh. She swayed back and forth with Clancy's slow jog and listened to her older brothers. They were talking about the friends they hadn't seen all summer. A little shiver of excitement ran down Sarah's spine. Her eyes sparkled. She forgot all about the scary flutterings she had felt at breakfast.

Friends! Girlfriends! A girl to play dolls with, to share with. Ever since Sarah could remember, she had dreamed of having a girlfriend. She had two older brothers and eight cousins. And every cousin was a boy! It seemed to Sarah as if Yonder Mountain produced only boys.

The sun whisked away the foggy mist of early morning. It warmed the night air that still lingered under the trees. It shone gently on the yellow and orange wildflowers that grew along the dirt road. But Sarah did not notice.

She was thinking about the girl who would become her friend. Sarah decided that her new friend would have blue eyes and black hair. She would have a happy smile. And she would like Sarah right away.

When they reached the schoolyard, Sarah looked for the girl of her daydreams. She saw many children in the yard. She saw some big boys and some little boys. She saw some tall boys and some short boys.

They called to Thomas and William. Thomas and William shouted back. They slid off Clancy and handed Sarah the reins.

"Just hitch him over there," Thomas told her, pointing to the back of the schoolhouse. "He'll eat the green grass there."

Sarah walked Clancy around to the back. She let him drink from a big tub of water. Then she hitched him beside some other horses. All the time, she watched the children who ran back and forth in the yard.

She saw her cousins. She saw the boys from Piney Ridge. She saw some boys she did not know. But she didn't see any girls. Slowly she walked back to the steps of the schoolhouse. Her new shoes made dragging marks in the ground, which had been worn bare by playing children.

"Come and climb this tree with us, Sarah," called William. Sarah shook her head.

"Come and play marbles, Sarah," called one of her cousins. "I've got a new cat's-eye marble."

Sarah shook her head.

"Come and play mumbletypeg, Sarah," called one of the boys from Piney Ridge. "You can use my knife."

Sarah shook her head and took EmmyLou out of her pinafore pocket. She didn't want to climb trees. She didn't want to play marbles. And she didn't want to play mumbletypeg. She wanted to play dolls.

The door opened behind her and a lovely lady appeared on the steps. Sarah stared at the crisp white shirt and trim skirt that just covered shiny leather shoes. She stared at the soft brown hair that was swept loosely up into a neat bun. Her mouth opened slowly.

But before she could say anything, William grabbed her arm. He yanked her into the line that was quickly forming in front of the steps.

"Do you want to get in trouble? That's Mrs. Walker," he whispered. "When she rings the bell, you're supposed to get in line!" Sarah barely heard him. She was pushed along by the moving line of boys. She found herself inside a large room that smelled faintly of chalk dust. On two sides were large windows, open to the mountain air. Through the center were rows of desks.

In the front, on a wooden platform, stood Mrs. Walker. And she was looking right at Sarah.

## Chapter Two
# A Friend for Sarah

Sarah blinked. The boys paired off and found their desks. Desk lids banged as the boys put away their things. The room seemed very big and very full of boys.

"Sarah and Jonathan," Mrs. Walker was saying, "you may take the seats right down here."

Sarah heard a noise behind her. She turned and saw a towheaded boy slightly smaller than herself. He followed her to the front and slid in beside her.

"You two are my only first graders," Mrs. Walker said. She smiled at them. "That makes you special, doesn't it?"

Sarah looked into Mrs. Walker's kind blue eyes. Suddenly she felt warm and happy. An answering smile lit her face. "Yes, ma'am."

Jonathan didn't smile. He sat stiffly at the desk, hands folded in front of him.

"Why don't you look through your desks," Mrs. Walker said quietly, "while I get the others settled in. We'll talk later."

Sarah opened her desk eagerly. She took out a slate and a single piece of chalk. In no time she was drawing a spiky "A" on the slate. Out of the corner of her eye she saw Jonathan watching her. After a while he opened his desk and gingerly took out his slate. He watched her draw a firm, round "O." He copied it carefully and neatly.

"Do you know your ABC's too?" Sarah asked.

He shook his head and looked down at his slate.

"Never you mind," Sarah said. "I learned from my brothers. I will teach you."

Mrs. Walker came to the front and led the pledge to the flag. Then she asked if anyone had any prayer requests.

Sarah listened to the requests. Just as Mrs. Walker was about to pray, Sarah's hand shot up.

"Yes, Sarah?"

Sarah blurted out, "Can we pray for another girl to come to school?"

A boy in the back hooted. Mrs. Walker silenced him with a look. "Yes, Sarah," she said gently, "we can."

Sarah let out her breath slowly. She bowed her head and listened as Mrs. Walker's voice calmed the room. The prayer sounded just right.

She and Jonathan talked quietly when Mrs. Walker was not working with them. He told her that he was an only child.

"You don't have any brothers or sisters?" Sarah was surprised. She couldn't imagine being without her Thomas and her William.

He shook his head.

"Do you know anyone here?" Sarah asked, wide-eyed.

Jonathan shook his head again. "Only you," he said shyly.

Sarah no longer felt lost in the big room. The buzz of reciting voices droned in the room. She put down her slate and listened as class after class met on the bench in front of her desk.

When it was time for recess, Sarah was surprised. The morning had gone quickly. She and Jonathan joined the others as they rushed outside. Sarah tucked up her skirts. She ran as fast as she could to the trees that ringed the clearing. She was heading for the tree that William and his friend had climbed. Two of the older boys were right behind her.

She reached the tree first and swung herself up. One of the boys caught her foot.

"This is our tree," he said. "Get down."

Sarah kicked her foot hard. "This is not your tree. It belongs to everyone. If you want to come up, come on."

"Ow," the boy said. He shook his hand. "That hurt. You'd better not kick me again."

Sarah frowned. "Then don't pull on me. I said there is room for you."

"Forget it," the boy said, walking away with his friend. "We're not playing with a girl."

Sarah shrugged and climbed higher in the tree. She settled down on a big branch and took EmmyLou out of her pocket.

She played with the doll for a while. Then she turned around to face the school. She saw

Jonathan standing by the steps. He was watching some boys play marbles. He moved too close to the boy who was shooting. The boy pushed him away. Jonathan slipped and fell into the game. Suddenly the bigger boys began to push and pull at him.

Sarah was out of the tree in a flash. She dashed into the huddle of boys, hitting them with EmmyLou. "You leave him alone!" she shouted.

"Ow!" said the boy who had pushed Jonathan. He put his arms up to fend off EmmyLou's floppy body. "Quit it!"

"Sarah!" Someone pinned Sarah's arms back. She couldn't see who it was, but she didn't like being held. She kicked back with her new shoes.

"Ow! Sarah!" Thomas groaned. "Don't you know better than to get into a fight at school?"

Sarah stopped. Thomas let her go and rubbed his leg. The other boys had grabbed their marbles

and scattered. Jonathan got up slowly. He looked as if he were about to cry.

"Hey," Thomas said. "They didn't mean any harm. Forget it. Go play with Sarah."

Sarah brushed off EmmyLou and smiled at Jonathan. "Do you like to climb?" she asked.

"Yes," he replied.

"Then come on," Sarah shouted happily. "Race you!"

She and Jonathan ran across the yard to the tree. Jonathan beat her by a foot and scrambled up ahead of her. They made it to the big branch and settled down.

"I'm sorry I went off without you," Sarah said. "I was just thinking of EmmyLou."

"EmmyLou?" Jonathan asked.

"My doll. Just look at her," Sarah said sadly. "She looks like she has been dragged through the brush backwards."

Jonathan looked. The doll dangled limply from Sarah's hand. Its pinafore hung off one arm. Stuffing drifted in frizzy white lumps from the doll's neck and head. Jonathan began to smile. Then he laughed out loud.

Sarah giggled. There might not be another girl at school, but Sarah had a friend just the same.

# Chapter Three
# Sarah Most Lively

Sarah loved the little school. She loved Mrs. Walker. She could hardly wait to get to school in the morning.

She did her lessons as neatly as she could, but sometimes they got a little mixed up. That was because Sarah listened to the other lessons. By the end of October, Sarah knew where to find India on the map. She knew what happened at Valley Forge. She knew how to spell *Christian* and *latitude* and *treasure*. But Sarah did not know how to do her first grade sums.

"Sarah, it's good to be interested in what is going on around you," Mrs. Walker said. "But you must do your own work first."

Sarah tried. She really did. But still she couldn't keep from listening to the upper grades. On Monday she stretched way over to see Luke Anderson's book. She slipped and knocked Jonathan out of his seat. Mrs. Walker shook her head as she helped Jonathan up.

On Wednesday Sarah put ink in the water bucket. She wanted to watch it spread like it had done in the sixth grade science lesson. Mrs. Walker was not happy. She sent Sarah to the stream for a clean bucket of water.

But when Sarah scrambled the fourth grade leaf collection to see if she could put it back together again, Mrs. Walker frowned. This time Mrs. Walker did not say, "It is good to be interested in things, Sarah."

She did not say anything for a while. When she spoke at last, she said, "Sarah, you are . . . most lively!"

And Sarah spent the afternoon sitting in the corner.

Gloom settled over Sarah's day. Her small face lost its bright glow. She sat as still as a spring fawn. She bent her head to hide her eyes. She didn't want to look at Thomas and William. She didn't want them to look at her.

When the class went to recess, Sarah felt someone stop close to her. Sarah didn't look up, even when something was pressed into her hand.

After the room was quiet, she opened her hand. There in her palm lay a tiny carved acorn doll. Her bottom lip trembled. Tears began to race down her dusty cheeks.

Mrs. Walker came back inside to speak to Sarah. "Why, Sarah," she said. Sarah flew into the open arms. Mrs. Walker held her until the sobs settled into hiccups.

"I'm sorry, Sarah," she said gently. "But we have many students here, from first grade to sixth. They all need my time."

Sarah sniffed and wiped her eyes. She knew how busy Mrs. Walker was. There were so many things to teach. And there was never enough time in the school day. "I promise I won't be lively again," she said quietly.

Mrs. Walker smiled. "Being lively can be good or it can be bad, Sarah," she said. "You must be lively doing the right things. You should think about what will happen before you do something."

"I will," Sarah said.

And she tried. She really tried. But quite often Sarah found herself on the stool in the corner. She learned to sit quietly, whispering to herself, "Not so lively, Sarah!"

Other children sat on the stool from time to time. Sarah began to understand what Mrs. Walker meant by "too lively." But it was only when the Clanton boys came to school that she really understood.

They came in the middle of the morning. Sarah felt the change in the classroom before she knew what was wrong. She turned to look. She saw two big boys. They were standing in the back with big grins on their faces.

"Harvest's done, Teacher," the biggest one said. "Ma sent us to git some larnin'."

"I've been expecting you, boys," Mrs. Walker said. "Take the two seats by the window."

Sarah swung back to stare at Mrs. Walker. Her voice sounded different. It was no louder than before, but it sounded stronger, much stronger.

The two boys settled in the seats. They did not listen to the lesson which began again in the front. Instead, they looked around the classroom. One of them saw Sarah staring and made a face. Sarah whipped back around and bent her head over her slate.

The schoolroom did not feel the same. It wasn't safe any more. Trouble seemed to be in

the air. Sarah felt it. So did the other children. And so did Mrs. Walker.

For days the classes went on as usual. The big boys did what they were told, but Sarah didn't like the way they did it. At family prayer time one night, Sarah prayed for Mrs. Walker and the big boys.

"They are just too lively," she told her mother.

"Have they disobeyed Mrs. Walker?" Pa asked.

Sarah shook her head. "But they don't really obey. Not the way we are supposed to."

"I see," said Pa. "Who are the boys?"

"Lijah and Trace Clanton," Thomas said.

"The Clanton boys," Pa said quietly. He looked at Ma. "I need to ride over to Four Corners tomorrow," he said. "I'll stop in at school."

The next day Sarah could hardly keep her eyes on her book. She kept glancing out of the window.

Pa came about noon. Mrs. Walker sent the children out to eat their lunches under the brightly colored trees. They stayed out a long time. Sarah and Jonathan sat on a huge stump facing the schoolhouse and watched the door. At last Pa came out.

He waved to Sarah and got on his horse. Sarah ran to stand beside Mrs. Walker. "Thank you, sir," Mrs. Walker said to Pa.

Sarah watched them both, puzzled. Nothing else was said. The day went on like any other day. But from then on one or another of the children's fathers just happened to drop by the school during the daytime.

Thomas was the one who told Sarah what was going on. "They're keeping an eye on the boys," he said. "There's trouble brewing—just you wait and see."

# Chapter Four
# Trouble Brewing

Sarah and Jonathan sat on the back steps. They were watching the Clanton boys chop firewood. The ring of the big axes mingled with the shouts of playing children. Chips flew as the shining blades came down again and again.

At last the boys stopped to rest. Sarah and Jonathan darted forward to scoop up the sweet-smelling chips. It didn't take long to fill Sarah's apron with the chips. Then they hurried back to their tree.

"Why do you want to stuff EmmyLou with the chips?" Jonathan asked. He was only half interested. His eyes were on the foot race that the second graders were starting.

"Because she lost most of her stuffing, remember?" Sarah replied. "Besides, the chips will make her smell sweet all winter. Don't you just love the smell of fresh wood?"

There was no reply. Sarah looked back. Jonathan was standing beside the starting line. She watched silently as one of the second graders pulled him into the race. The leader shouted, and the racers took off.

Sarah blinked. Then she looked again. Jonathan was running two feet ahead of the second graders! At the end of the race, the boys gathered around him. They clapped him on the back. "He's a runner," they shouted.

Sarah stood still. Jonathan trotted back to her, joy lighting his face. Sarah looked down at the chips in her apron. Then she looked at Jonathan. "You go run, Jonathan," she said cheerfully. "I'll stuff EmmyLou."

But Sarah didn't stuff EmmyLou right then. She put the chips into a secret hollow in the tree. She climbed as high as she could. The red, yellow, and orange leaves trembled around her. She shook the slender branches as hard as she could. Leaves showered to the ground. Only then did Sarah feel better.

She found a sturdy branch and sat down. She looked up at the bright blue of the cloudless sky. "Please send a girl for me to play with, Lord," she prayed. "Please."

Finally Sarah came down from the tree. She stuffed EmmyLou with the chips. She didn't have quite enough. So she went back to the chopping block to get some to finish.

The Clanton boys were not there. Sarah gathered another apronful of chips and started back to the old tree. Just before she reached the corner of the schoolhouse, she looked back.

Lijah and Trace were coming out the back door. They were snickering and whispering to each other. As Sarah watched, Lijah couldn't hold back his laughter any longer. He stumbled down the steps, laughing loudly. Trace followed him quickly. He tried to hush his brother. When he looked up and saw Sarah, he stamped his feet and made an awful face.

Sarah ran back to the front. Mrs. Walker was still inside. The boys couldn't have done anything without her seeing them. Still, Sarah didn't like it. She just knew those boys were up to something. Whatever it was, it was no good.

The next morning, frost sparkled on the browning grass. Ma bundled Sarah and her brothers into thick jackets and woolen mittens. The children rushed out the door. They blew into the air to make tiny cloudlike puffs of breath.

Old Clancy stamped in the yard, blowing clouds of his own. For once, the old horse was ready to go. Sarah got on behind her brothers, and Clancy started off in a spine-jolting trot.

The Clanton boys were the first students at school. A roaring fire burned in the big stove. Fresh firewood was stacked in the woodbox. After they had hung their things in the cloakroom, the children warmed themselves at the stove. Then Mrs. Walker called them to their seats.

Joshua Singleton's father stopped by about an hour later. He checked the woodbox and nodded. He waved to Mrs. Walker and winked at the children. Then he went on his way.

Sarah saw the looks the Clanton boys gave each other. Her cheerful smile disappeared. She tried to watch them, but Mrs. Walker told her to turn around. Sarah bent her head over her lessons.

Behind her she heard a scuffling noise. She listened so hard that she thought her ears were standing out from her head. She saw Mrs. Walker look up. Then there was the scrape and clunk of logs being dropped.

Sarah relaxed. Lijah was just getting wood for the stove. The stove door clanked open. The fire whispered and crackled. Lijah slammed the door and hurried back to his seat.

Sarah began to do her sums slowly and carefully. Suddenly an explosion splintered the quiet of the schoolroom. The boys jumped up. Slates shattered against the floor. Some boys flung themselves under their desks. Some raced for the windows. Some charged out the back door. Sarah sat frozen in her seat. She could only stare at Mrs. Walker's shocked face.

The room slowly quieted down. Sarah heard funny noises coming from behind her. She turned, her heart still pounding. Lijah and Trace lay across their desks, gasping with laughter.

"Boys!" Mrs. Walker's voice crackled with anger.

Everything became still. The Clanton boys stopped laughing and sat up. They looked at the teacher's face and frowned.

"I just threw a few rocks in the stove. Didn't hurt anything." Lijah's voice was sullen.

"That's not the point." Mrs. Walker settled the class and gave new lessons in a tight, hard voice. When the children were working, she marched to the back.

The children watched wide-eyed as Mrs. Walker grabbed one Clanton with her right hand and one Clanton with her left hand. She marched the protesting boys outside.

They were gone for a long time. The children scribbled their lessons, listening as hard as they could. But they heard nothing. After a while, the boys came back in quietly. They took their seats and reached for their slates. For the first time since they had come to school, the boys began to do their lessons. Sarah's eyes widened.

At last Mrs. Walker came back in. She looked just like she had looked before she had hustled the boys out. Every hair was in place, and her dress was as neat as a pin. She went to her desk and looked over the classroom. The children stared back at her.

"There's work to be done," she said gently. "First grade, come to the front."

The noise of working students buzzed behind Sarah. She stood up and followed Jonathan. The tightness eased from her throat. Everything was going to be all right.

# Chapter Five
# Forgiven

Ice crackled under Clancy's hooves. Icicles hung from the tree branches. The cold wind nipped at Sarah's face. She shivered and pressed her face to William's back.

When they reached the school yard, Sarah slid down quickly. She hurried inside to hang up her coat. The stove was burning, but no one was in the room. Sarah dropped EmmyLou on her desk. The hot stove reminded her of her potato. She went back to get the potato out of her lunch pail.

The back door opened. Lijah came in, carrying firewood. Trace followed. He closed the door against the wintry wind. Lijah crossed the room and dropped the firewood into the woodbox. Trace stopped by Sarah's desk.

"Well, here's little lively Sarah," he drawled. "And here's her dolly." He picked up EmmyLou and tossed her in the air.

"Put her down!" Sarah started toward him.

"Catch, Lije!" Trace called. He threw the doll to his brother.

Sarah reached up, but EmmyLou curved high over her head. She wheeled around. "Catch it, Lije!" Trace shouted again as EmmyLou flew across the room.

Lijah had opened the stove to put in some chunks of firewood. He looked up, startled. Before he could drop the firewood, EmmyLou bounced off his arm.

The doll hit the open door. A leg flopped into the fire. Lijah jumped back as the doll blazed into flames.

"EmmyLou!" Sarah shrieked. She ran to the stove.

Lijah caught her and pulled her back. "It's gone," he said roughly. "Can't you see?"

Sarah saw. The smell of burning wool filled the air. Sarah began to hit and kick at Lijah.

He held her down. "It was an accident," he said. "An accident."

Then Mrs. Walker was there, separating them. Sarah went to her seat and put her head down.

"What happened here?" Mrs. Walker asked.

"Trace threw the doll to me," Lijah said. "It fell in the stove by accident."

"Is this true, Sarah?" Mrs. Walker asked.

"Yes." Sarah raised her head. She sat up. "It was an accident."

"Very well. You know not to play in the schoolroom, boys. I'll take care of you later," Mrs. Walker said. She went to Sarah. "I know the doll meant a lot to you, Sarah. It is good of you to forgive the boys for playing."

"Yes, ma'am."

When Mrs. Walker was gone, Sarah looked at Trace. "But I don't forgive you," she said to herself. "I don't forgive you at all."

Sarah went through the day woodenly. She didn't smile once, not even when Jonathan drew a funny picture on his slate. From time to time, Mrs. Walker gave her a troubled look, but she didn't say anything.

In a few days Sarah felt better. She played with Jonathan and the other boys. She played the games her brothers had taught her. And she tried not to think of EmmyLou.

It was only when she looked at Trace and Lijah that she let herself remember. So she didn't look at them at all. It was as if the two boys were not in school at all. Not for Sarah.

On the first of December, the children drew names for Christmas gifts. Each child was to bring a gift for the person whose name he drew from Mrs. Walker's bowl.

Mrs. Walker passed around the bowl. She started with Sarah. Carefully, Sarah chose one of the slips. Each child took a folded slip of paper. "Now, don't open them until everyone has drawn," said Mrs. Walker.

When everyone had drawn a name, the children unfolded the slips. Sarah read the name on her piece of paper. Then she crumpled the paper. She let it fall on the floor. On the way home, Thomas and William tried to get each other to tell whose name they had drawn. Sarah said nothing. The boys got Ma and Pa to help them start making gifts. Still Sarah said nothing.

At last it was one week before Christmas. The big basket in front of the classroom was overflowing with gifts. Thomas and William counted them every day. All the gifts were in the basket but one.

That day, when Mrs. Walker read from the Bible, she did not read from Luke 2. Instead she chose Luke 23.

"At Christmas, we think of Jesus as a baby. Sometimes we forget about Jesus as a man," she said. "It is good to remember what He did for us."

Sarah listened as Mrs. Walker read about the cross. She listened as Mrs. Walker read about what men did to Jesus. And she listened as Mrs. Walker read His words, "Father, forgive them; for they know not what they do."

"Isn't it wonderful," Mrs. Walker said gently, "that Jesus forgave us when we were still sinners! He forgave everything. Everything."

Sarah was quiet for the rest of the day. When it was time to leave, Mrs. Walker stopped her. "I found this on the floor after we drew names. I think it is yours, Sarah," she said quietly. She opened her hand and held out a tiny slip of paper.

That night Sarah sat through devotions silently. When it came time for her to pray, she burst into tears.

Pa took her in his arms. "Now, what's been bothering Sarah?" he asked.

Sarah held out the tattered piece of paper. Ma smoothed it out and read the name, "Trace Clanton."

"I hated him." The words tumbled out of Sarah, one over another. "I wouldn't forgive him for killing EmmyLou. I wouldn't make him a present. Oh, Pa, will God ever forgive *me?*"

"Yes, Sarah," Pa said. "But you have to ask Him. No one else can do it for you."

Pa held Sarah as she prayed. When she lifted her head, her wet eyes were no longer sad. Then she thought about the presents. She put her hand to her mouth. "But our Christmas presents are supposed to be in the basket tomorrow. How will I make a present before tomorrow?"

# Chapter Six
# A Special Christmas

"I don't have time to make a gift for Trace," Sarah said. "Oh, what can I do?"

"I think I can take care of that," Ma said. She went into her bedroom and came back with a basket.

In the basket were skeins of blue and white wool. Ma reached underneath the wool. She took out dark blue mittens. She took out dark blue socks. She took out a muffler patterned in snowflakes.

"Mrs. Walker told us Trace didn't have a present in the basket," she said. "I thought it best to be prepared."

"Oh, Ma," Sarah said. "They are pretty."

"I hope they are not too pretty," Ma said, "or Trace won't wear them."

Sarah thought of the thin coat that Trace wore. She remembered seeing him bring wood in with his bare hands. "He and his brother come early to light the fire," Sarah said. "I think he will like them."

She fingered the mittens. "But Mrs. Walker said we should make our own gifts. I have done nothing."

"The muffler still needs fringe," Ma said. "There's lots of yarn left."

Soon Sarah was busy finishing the muffler. The dark gloom that had spoiled her Christmas was gone. As she worked, snowflakes began to drift past the window.

William saw them first. "Ma! Sarah!" he called. "It's snowing!"

They went to watch the whirling flakes. The flakes came down faster and faster. They were white against the dark blue of the sky.

"Just like the snowflakes on the muffler," Sarah said softly. "Look, Ma."

The next morning the world was all sparkling white hills and bright blue sky. Pa took the children to school in the little sled. The three children huddled on the back seat. A bearskin rug kept them as warm as toast. They sang at the top of their lungs as the sled runners whisked along the powdery snow.

Sarah was the first one out when they reached the school. She took her carefully wrapped gift in and placed it with the others. Mrs. Walker smiled at her. "Thank you, Sarah," she said. "I've been praying for you."

Sarah smiled back. She was surprised at how good it felt to smile. "Merry Christmas, Mrs. Walker."

For the first time, Sarah looked at the gifts in the basket. She touched the one with her name

on it. It was soft. Sarah went to her desk, still smiling.

"Hey, Sarah!" Jonathan told her when she sat down.

Sarah gave him a startled look.

"I'm glad you are back," Jonathan said.

"But I have been here," she replied.

"No, you haven't," Jonathan said, looking old and wise. "I'm glad your happy look is back."

Sarah's brown eyes twinkled even brighter. "So am I."

At recess the boys divided into teams and made snowforts. Sarah was on Jonathan's team. They made snowballs until their hands were cold even in the woolen mittens. When the other team launched an attack, they were ready.

Sarah laughed as Jonathan leaped from wall to wall, flinging snowballs.

"More, Sarah, more," he called excitedly.

Sarah quickly formed more snowballs. She crawled along the wall and handed them up to Jonathan one at a time. Before the balls were all gone, Mrs. Walker rang the bell.

The fight was called a tie.

Inside, the children found hot chocolate bubbling on the stove. The smell of baking potatoes filled the air.

"Um, I'm hungry," Sarah said.

"Before we eat, we should pass out the gifts," Mrs. Walker said. "Sarah, since you are the only girl, why don't we start with you?"

Sarah went to the front. She reached into the big basket and took out her package. She took it to Trace and laid it on the desk. "Merry Christmas, Trace," she said. "I'm sorry I got so mad at you about EmmyLou."

Everyone watched as Trace opened the present. He touched the soft wool in wonder. He cleared his throat. "Thank you, Sarah," he mumbled.

Each person gave his gift. And the class waited while the gift was opened. Jonathan got a whimmydiddle from William. Thomas got a new slingshot. Each present was greeted with cheerful comments from the rest of the class.

Finally there was only one present left. Sarah knew it was hers. She looked around the class. Lijah was the only one who had not given out a present.

He walked to the front of the room. Sarah had forgotten how tall he was. His arms and legs were clumsy, but none of the children laughed. They waited in silence. Sarah held her breath.

Lijah put the present in front of her. "I drew your name," he said, "but Trace hired out to buy the cloth. Ma made it. She said she always wanted to have a girl to make pretties for."

Sarah opened the package carefully. Inside lay a lovely cloth doll. Her eyes were brown like Sarah's. Her hair was brown like Sarah's. She had on a blue-flowered dress. Over it was a white pinafore with deep pockets.

Lijah shuffled his feet. "Don't you like it?" he blurted out.

Sarah held the doll to her chest. "Yes, I like her. Thank you, Lije. You, too, Trace."

Sarah named the new doll Lizzie. "You'll have to be my friend, Lizzie," she whispered. "At least until another girl comes to live on Yonder Mountain."

# Chapter Seven
# The Snows of Winter

Snow covered the mountain. It lay along the hollows in white swirls of powder. It piled up along the ridges in windswept drifts.

The sled skimmed over the surface of the snow. The bells on Old Clancy's harness jingled. Sarah cuddled deep in the bearskin rug and put her feet on a box of bricks. Ma had warmed the bricks on the stove and tucked them into the sled at the last moment.

But Sarah couldn't stay still long. She pushed herself up to get a good look at the frozen landscape.

"Be still, Sarah," Thomas complained. "You're freezing us."

"Pa," William called. "Sarah's being too lively."

"Settle down, Sarah," Pa told her.

"This is like being in a cocoon," Sarah said, settling back down.

"Or the inside of a bear's belly," William replied.

Sarah giggled. Thomas chuckled. Then the three of them were laughing loudly.

"What's so funny?" Pa said. He looked back at the three pairs of eyes that showed just above the fur.

"I said we are in a cocoon," Sarah said. "But William said we are in a bear's belly."

Pa's big laugh rumbled from inside his fur blanket. He waved toward the snow. "What do you think the snow looks like, William?"

William thought a moment. "Ma's white quilt," he said, "in the morning after it has been tumbled about."

"It does not," Sarah said. "It looks like miles and miles of sugar spilled by a giant."

"What about you, Thomas?" Pa asked.

"Sand," Thomas replied. "White sand, like in the desert."

"It's feathers . . ."

"It's a thousand polar bears taking naps."

When the sled stopped in front of the little schoolhouse, the children were still trying to think of new ways to tell about the snow. Mrs. Walker listened to them as they hung up their coats. They went to their seats, flushed and excited.

"Who else can tell us about snow?" Mrs. Walker said.

In seconds, words were flying about as thickly as the snowflakes that had fallen last night. Mrs. Walker wrote them down. When the children were finished, she read the words back to them. Then she went to her bookshelf. She selected a small book of poems to read aloud.

Sarah listened with her eyes closed. The words made pictures in her head, beautiful pictures. When Mrs. Walker closed the book, Sarah sighed.

The room was warm with good feelings. Sarah took out the book that Ma had given her. Thomas had read it. So had William. Now it was Sarah's turn.

The book was an old friend. Sarah knew the pictures in the book as well as she knew her name. It delighted her that she could read the words by herself. When Mrs. Walker called for the first grade, Sarah beat Jonathan to the bench. She read in a firm voice, without stumbling over one word.

Mrs. Walker smiled. "Good, Sarah."

When the children got home, apple pie was cooling on the back of the stove. The tangy, sweet smell filled the small house. Sarah took a deep breath. Her stomach rumbled. She hurried to set the table.

After supper, Sarah helped Ma with the dishes. When they finished, Pa got the big Bible from the mantel. They all sat around the table as Pa read. Sarah did not wiggle, not even once. Hers was the first hand up for prayer. She prayed for Mrs. Walker and Trace and Lijah. Then she prayed for a girl to come to Yonder Mountain. And after she had prayed, she listened to every word of the other prayers.

Thomas and William stayed at the kitchen table to do their homework. Pa went out to the stable. Ma took one of the lamps to the small table beside her rocking chair. She pulled up a huge basket of wool.

"Come, Sarah," she said.

Sarah sat on a stool beside Ma. She took two wooden paddles out of the basket. One side of each paddle was smooth wood. The other side was covered with lots of short, stiff wire. Sarah pulled off a thick hunk of wool and placed it on the wire side of one paddle. Then she used the other paddle to pull the wool.

Whish, whish went the paddles. Back and forth, back and forth. Sarah liked carding the wool because she could watch everything else that was going on. When the wool was firmly in the paddle, she could even get up and walk around. Tonight she was too wiggly to sit still.

She got up and went to the table. She stood behind William and watched him struggle with his spelling.

"Patience," he said out loud. "*P-a,* pa, *s-h-u-n*—"

"That's not right," said Sarah.

"Ma!" William called. "Sarah's bothering me."

"Sarah," Ma said.

Sarah sighed, but she went to sit on the stool beside Ma. She swung her knees back and forth

as she carded the wool. Whish, whish. Thump, thump.

The door opened and Pa came in. He hung his heavy winter coat on a peg by the door. Sarah watched as he dropped Clancy's harness on the floor and warmed his hands at the fire.

"I put the beeswax on the back of the stove, Pa," she said. "It should be warm enough by now."

Pa found it and sat down at the table with the boys. He put some of the wax on a cloth and began to rub the leather straps of the harness.

Sarah yawned. To keep herself awake, she tried to sort out all the smells of home as her hands went back and forth, back and forth. Apple and wax, biscuits and wood smoke, warm leather and lamp oil.

The lamps made islands of light in the darkening room. Sarah watched the leather straps begin to gleam under her father's hands.

He rubbed the beeswax back and forth. Swish, swish.

Sarah's eyelids felt heavy. The paddles in her hands moved back and forth. Whish, whish. Slower and slower. Whish . . . whish.

"Sarah," Ma said. She took the paddles from Sarah's still hands. "Bedtime, Sarah."

# Chapter Eight
# Maple Sugar

Winter reached the stage Ma called Wet Wool. The winter sun brightened. The snow began to melt. Water began to gurgle under the sheets of ice that covered the mountain streams.

It was still cold. The children bundled up when they went outside. When they came inside again, their woolen mittens, coats, and stockings were wet with melting snow.

The prickly smell of wet wool filled the house. Ma threatened to toss the batch of them into the stable with Old Clancy. Sarah and her

brothers laughed. They knew that Ma didn't mean it.

The quiet days at school changed. The long winter months had been good months for learning. Now the stir in the air left the children restless. Their gaze was often fixed on the windows, not on their slates.

The trees budded. Pa pointed out the green swellings one morning. "Spring's on its way," he said. Sarah was beside herself with excitement. At school nothing seemed to go right for her. She couldn't find her reader. She spilled her ink. She tripped over her own feet on the way to the reading bench.

For the first time in quite a while, Mrs. Walker frowned at Sarah. "You're too lively today, Sarah," she said. "Slow down and think."

Sarah felt as if her brain had been wrapped in the same wool she had carded all winter. She wanted to be out in the soft breezes that made the willow branches dance. "Spring is coming," she told everyone who would listen.

But the next week snow fell again in the mountains. On Saturday morning, the wind whistling around the eaves woke Sarah before dawn. She climbed down the ladder from the loft bedroom that she shared with the boys. When Pa got up to do his chores, he found Sarah in the front room. Her nose was pressed against the cold pane.

"It snowed, Pa," Sarah said sadly. "Spring isn't here after all."

Pa looked out the window. His eyes began to twinkle. "Well, Miss Sarah," he said. "This is the kind of snow you might just like."

Sarah brushed her tangled hair away from her face. She looked up at him. "But I'm tired of snow, Pa."

Pa tweaked her nose. "This snow is special."

"How, Pa?" Sarah asked.

"It's a sugar snow," Pa said. "You remember all those buckets Thomas and William helped me make last fall? This week we went into the woods. We drove strips of bamboo into the trunks of the biggest and best maple trees. The warm weather started the sap running."

"But won't it stop now?" Sarah asked.

"Nope. This late snow will make the sap sweeter. It's going to be a good year for maple sugar."

"Maple sugar!" Sarah's mouth watered as she thought of the thick chunks of brown sugar. "We're going to make our own?"

"Yep. This'll be our first year at sugaring off," Pa said. "We'll have stacks of sugar, just like the Stanfords and the Brightons had last spring!"

"When, Pa?"

"Right now," Pa said. "Go wake up your brothers, Miss Sarah! Look lively, now!"

The boys came out of bed, blinking and yawning. But when Sarah told them about the sugar snow, they forgot all about being sleepy. They raced for the ladder.

Ma caught them halfway down. "Back up, boys! No breakfast until you are dressed!"

Pa chuckled. "Better obey, boys. I'll meet you in the barn."

The children hardly noticed what they ate. They finished as quickly as possible. Thomas and William left as soon as they were excused. Sarah looked at the door longingly as she began to clear the table.

Ma smiled. "Just leave those, Sarah. I can manage today."

"You mean it, Ma?" Sarah asked hopefully.

"I mean it," she replied.

Sarah grabbed her coat. She was out the door before Ma could change her mind. She caught up with the boys in the barn. "I can go, too," she told them.

Pa had hitched Old Clancy to the sled. "You'll have to ride up front with me, Sarah," he said. "The back is full of buckets."

Sarah climbed in. Pa clucked and Old Clancy plodded off. The first bucket was dropped off a hundred yards from the barn. Thomas hung it on its bamboo spout. William got to do the next one.

Pa handed Sarah the third bucket. "Look sharp, Sarah. See if you can find the third tree."

Sarah looked and looked. She saw mountain laurel and loblolly pine. She saw hemlock and sweet gum. She saw maple trees and more maple trees. She looked for the biggest maple tree around. And there was the bamboo spout.

"I see it," she said. She held up her skirts and picked her way through the snow to the tree. Carefully she hung her bucket on the bamboo spout. "Done, Pa!"

They hung fifty buckets on fifty trees. When they had finished, they were back at the barn.

"We made a circle, Pa," Sarah said. "Round and round and round and back here."

"Makes the trees easy to find," Pa said. "Remember how the first tree was marked?"

Sarah nodded.

"I marked it," Thomas said, grinning. "If you sight from the first tree, you can find the next."

"And from that tree, you can find the third." William's grin was just as big.

Sarah stared at the boys. "You mean you knew where the third tree was all along?"

Pa chuckled. Thomas and William began to laugh.

"You!" Sarah screeched. She took off after the boys as they ran to the house. "I'll get you two! Just you wait!"

# Chapter Nine
# Sugaring Off

Sarah and her brothers told everyone at school about the maple sugar. They told them about the sugaring off that was set for Friday night. "Everyone is invited," Thomas said.

All week Sarah helped her mother clean the house. By Friday the house, the barn, and the storage shed were sparkling clean. Sarah went to school with aching muscles, but she didn't care. She was too excited.

"Are you coming, Mrs. Walker?" she asked for the third time.

"Yes, Sarah," Mrs. Walker said. "I wouldn't miss it for the world."

Sarah turned and bumped into Trace. "You coming, Trace?"

Trace gave her a funny look. "To some old sugaring-off party? Why should I?"

Sarah was surprised. "Because we want you to come, that's why."

"You do?" It was Trace's turn to sound surprised.

"Yes, will you?"

"Maybe," Trace replied gruffly. "Maybe not."

Sarah had to be satisfied with his answer. She sat down beside Jonathan. "Are you coming?" she asked.

"Ma said we could. She said she hadn't been to a sugaring off since she was little," Jonathan replied.

Sarah barely kept her mind on her lessons. At the end of the day, she was the first one in line. She was into the sled almost before Pa stopped Old Clancy. "Is everything ready, Pa?" she asked.

"Buckets emptied, pails full, fire's hot," Pa replied. "There'll be maple sugar tonight."

Thomas and William climbed aboard. They settled down beside Sarah and waved to their friends. "See you tonight," they called.

Old Clancy couldn't move fast enough for Sarah. Pa had to stop her from climbing out and running ahead of the sled. "We'll get there soon enough, Sarah," he told her.

And they did. Sarah found that Ma had finished most of the work. She had fixed venison with fluffy potatoes and thick gravy. A big pot of leather beans steamed on the stove. From the oven came the smell of fresh baked bread.

"I thought everybody was bringing food," Pa teased. "Why, you've cooked enough for an army."

"I won't be caught without enough," Ma said firmly. She checked the food again and relaxed. "I guess I have overdone it a mite."

"Won't hurt," Pa said. He gave her a hug. "Tonight is special."

Sarah agreed. She helped to set the tables in between skipping to the windows to look down the road. Near dusk, she saw the first lantern. "They're coming!" she called. "They're coming!"

Mrs. Walker came with her husband. He was big and tall. He shook Sarah's hand and said, "I've heard a lot about you, Sarah-most-lively."

Sarah stared up at the big man and forgot to speak. Mrs. Walker gave her a gentle push. "There's someone else at the door, Sarah. I'll help your mother."

Sarah nodded. She opened the door to Jonathan, his mother, and his father. She greeted them with delight. "Come in, come in."

Soon the small house was packed. The Andersons were there, the Trasks, the McBrides, and more kept coming. Even Trace and Lijah came with their mother. "Thank you for the doll," Sarah told Mrs. Clanton.

"It was fun to make," Mrs. Clanton said. A smile lit her worn face. "I always wanted a girl. All I got was two boys, wild as the March wind."

"They're strong boys," Sarah said.

"That they are, child," Mrs. Clanton agreed. "And since their Pa died, they've taken right good care of me."

The boys disappeared into the crowd. Sarah took Mrs. Clanton to meet Ma. She peered into the boiling pots. "Is it ready?" she asked.

"It will be," Ma replied. She shooed Sarah out of the kitchen.

The planks that had been set up in the living room for tables were loaded with food. Everyone had brought something special. They had brought their own plates and glasses so the supper would not be a burden on Ma and Pa. Sarah liked the bright look of the mismatched sets. It reminded her of Ma's flower border in full bloom.

"Get the boys in, Sarah," called Ma. "It's time to eat."

Supper was good. It was the best Sarah had eaten since the circuit-riding preacher had come in the summer. But nothing could beat maple sugar. Sarah ate lightly, saving room for the sweets.

The tables were cleared and everyone was having a good time when Ma called, "It's ready!"

The children lined up at the door with plates in hand. Ma ladled the thick syrup into the plates. As each plate was filled, its owner dashed out the back door into the snow.

They scooped up handfuls of clean snow and sprinkled it on the plates of syrup. It hardened quickly. Then they ate the maple sugar carefully, chunk by chunk.

Sarah waited until the boys had been served. Then she took her plate outside. The snow around the door was scuffled. She looked

around. Over the door was a fluffy mound of clean snow. She held her plate carefully and tried to reach it.

"Hold on." Trace spoke right behind her. "I'll get it."

He reached up and scooped a double handful of the snow. "There," he said. "That'll do it."

"Thanks," Sarah said.

"Forget it," Trace replied and hurried off.

Sarah ate slowly. She enjoyed every bite, more so because it was their sugar, from their land. She ate until she could hold no more.

When everyone had left, family by family, Sarah was too tired and sleepy to be sad. It had been just fine. Pa said they should do it again. Sarah agreed. "Next year," she said to herself. "Next year."

# Chapter Ten
# The Spelling Bee

"This will be the last snow," Pa said. "It'll soon be time for spring planting."

"Spring thaw is coming," Ma said, excitement in her voice. "Brother Parks will soon be here."

Sarah clapped. She liked the circuit-riding preacher. She liked the meetings. And there was something else. She looked at William. Every year Brother Parks gave a brand-new Bible to the best speller in the school. Every year William had tried his best to win the Bible. Every year he had failed.

That night William sat hunched over his speller. His lips moved as he silently spelled the letters. William worked hard at spelling. Sometimes he would copy verses from the family Bible. Sarah knew he wanted a Bible of his own to read and study.

Sarah loved William, and she wished she could help him. She was a good speller. When the others toed the mark for each grade's spelldown, Sarah had spelled right along with them. But she made sure she spelled the words in her mind instead of out loud.

"William," she whispered. "I could help you with your words."

William looked across the table at Sarah. "I really could use some help," he said. "I'm going to have to work hard to beat Willie and Joshua. They're really good."

Sarah pulled her chair close to her brother. He looked through the speller for words he thought she could say. By the time Ma called Sarah for bed, they had spelled through three word lists.

For the next two nights, the children worked on spelling. By the night before the Bee, Sarah was having trouble reading the longer words.

"I have to know the long ones," William said. "They are the tie-breakers."

"Sometimes Mrs. Walker uses long words from the Bible," Sarah said. "Why don't we study those?"

William got up and stretched to ease his cramped muscles. He walked stiffly over to the mantel and brought back the family Bible. He gently opened to the Psalms. Then he leafed backward to the Old Testament books that came first.

"Here's a good place to find words," he said. "I'm ready!"

Sarah ran her finger down the page until she came to a word that looked long enough for William. Again and again she found words and William spelled them. Ma let her stay up past her bedtime to help. When she finally called Sarah, the tired girl crept up the ladder to her bed in the loft. Below, William was still hunched over the speller.

The next morning, excitement tingled in the air. Some children chattered with their well-wishing friends. Others sat at their desks, heads still bent over open spellers.

When Brother Parks came in, the children closed their books and sat up tall. "Well, students," he said, "are you ready?"

"Yes, sir!" The class answered. Sarah was pleased to hear William's voice clearly.

"Then let's pray," the preacher said. The children bowed their heads. When Brother Parks finished, Sarah silently tagged on a prayer of her own. "Please, Lord, let William do his best."

Sarah and Jonathan had the best seats in the room. As first graders, they were not in the Spelling Bee. But each recited a poem for the preacher. Then two of the older boys read special stories they had written. Finally Mrs. Walker called for the class to toe the mark.

The boys got into a line facing Mrs. Walker and Brother Parks. Everyone was silent. Mrs. Walker called out the first word.

"Trust. I will trust in God."

"*T-r-u-s-t,*" spelled Joseph. "Trust."

For a while, no one missed a word. Then the words got harder. One by one, the boys stumbled over a word. And one by one, the boys sat down.

Sarah held her breath every time Mrs. Walker came to William. After a while there were only four boys left. William was one of them. Sarah just knew he could win. But, as the words got longer, she began to twist her hands.

"Mephibosheth," said Mrs. Walker. She said the name loudly and clearly.

William looked at Sarah and smiled. That was one of the long Bible words that Sarah had found for him. She had drilled him until he could spell it perfectly each time. Two of the boys went down on that word. Then it was William's turn.

He took a deep breath. "*M-e,* Me, *p-h-i-b,* phib, *o,* o, *s-h-e-t-h,* sheth, Mephibosheth."

Now only William and Henry Mason stood in front of the room. Mrs. Walker gave the two boys word after word. Neither boy made a mistake. Sarah didn't know the words. She frowned. Maybe she had not done enough for William!

Then Mrs. Walker called out, "Prudent."

It was Henry's turn. He spelled, "*P-r-u,* pru, *d-a-n-t,* dant."

Mrs. Walker shook her head. "William?"

"*P-r-u,* pru, *d-e-n-t,* dent," William spelled.

Henry sat down. Mrs. Walker gave one more word. Sarah didn't even hear William spell it. Her eyes were on Brother Parks. He had picked up the Bible and gone to stand beside Mrs. Walker. Mrs. Walker nodded to show that William had spelled the last word right. The class stood up, clapping wildly.

That night after prayer time, William got out his new Bible. After everyone had looked at it again, he got a pen and some ink.

"Stand here, Sarah," he said. He turned to the first page, where Brother Parks had written William's name. "Something needs to be added to this page in my Bible."

William dipped his pen in the ink. The lamp shone on his strong hand. It made the ink glisten as he formed the letters.

Next to his own name he wrote, "and Sarah Goodwin."

# Chapter Eleven
# A Time for Meeting

Brother Parks stayed in town for a week. School was out for spring planting. Fathers and sons plowed the ground during the day. At night the families met in the schoolhouse for the preaching.

Sarah had a question to ask Brother Parks. She was glad that he would be staying with them for the first night of his visit. But things did not work out the way Sarah expected.

People dropped by all during the day to speak to Brother Parks. When he wasn't busy with them, he was off somewhere with Pa. Even the boys got to talk to him, for they tagged along with the men.

But Sarah had work to do. Sarah helped her mother cook. She set the table. When supper was over, she cleared the table. She waited and waited for a chance to speak to the preacher.

At last she saw him go outside by himself. Sarah wiped her hands and followed him. She found him sitting on a stump. He had his Bible open and was reading aloud. Sarah stopped. Was there no time she could speak to him?

Sarah turned away.

"Sarah?"

She went back to him.

"Is there anything I can do for you, child?" he asked.

"Does God ever *not* answer a prayer?" she asked.

Brother Parks looked thoughtful. "Well, yes," he said. "Sometimes we ask for things for selfish reasons. Sometimes we ask for things God

knows are not good for us. God knows what is best, Sarah. Why do you ask?"

Sarah looked into the kind face. She squirmed a little, but she had to know. "I have prayed and prayed, and God has not answered my prayer," she blurted out. "I am beginning to wonder if He hears me."

"God hears your prayer," Brother Parks said. "Perhaps He doesn't think it is time to answer it yet."

"But it has been months and months and months," Sarah said.

"That long?" Brother Parks eyes twinkled. "And what have you been praying for so hard?"

"A girlfriend," Sarah said slowly. "I prayed for a girl to come to Yonder Mountain."

"I see." Brother Parks smiled. "God has His own timetable, Sarah. Why not just wait on Him?"

Sarah sighed. Wait. It seemed like that was what she did all the time. "Yes, sir."

As she turned to go, Brother Parks called her back. "Sarah?"

"Yes, sir?"

"Keep a sharp eye out tonight," he said. His eyes were twinkling more than ever. "God might answer your prayer sooner than you think."

"Yes, sir!"

Sarah hurried back inside to get ready. "What if Brother Parks is wrong?" she wondered. Doubt made her uneasy. Still, she dressed in her best. She found a pale blue satin ribbon and put it in her hair. She looked at herself in the mirror. She smoothed her dress.

"Sarah!" Ma called from below.

"I'm coming," Sarah called back. She took a deep breath and hurried down.

Brother Parks and Pa had already gone. Thomas had hitched Old Clancy to the wagon. Sarah climbed in beside Ma.

The sky had deepened to dark blue. Stars twinkled, clear and bright. The night air was still brisk. Sarah drew her shawl close. Her thoughts were not on the night. "Maybe," she said to herself. "Maybe."

They saw the lights before they reached the school. The schoolyard was lit by torches. The windows of the schoolhouse shone with the light of lamps and candles.

Many wagons and horses were already hitched outside the schoolhouse. And inside, the classroom was crowded with people. Sarah had no time to look around. She hurried after Ma. They found a place on the third row of desks, beside Granny Hazel.

Sarah squeezed in and began to look around. Mrs. Alderson had a new baby. So did Mrs. Taylor. The smaller kids were staring about the room, wide-eyed. Sarah smiled. She remembered how she had felt last meeting-time. She had come to William's and Thomas's school. Now it was hers as well.

Pa was sitting up front with Brother Parks and Mr. Edwards. They would take care of the singing and the offering. Brother Parks would be free to pray before preaching. Sarah smiled at her father. He looked tall and strong and handsome in his best pants and shirt.

There was a stir in the crowd as the doors opened. Someone else entered. Sarah craned her neck to see. She saw a woman and man that she didn't know. And she saw just the tip of a frilly sunbonnet. It was bobbing along beside the woman.

"Who are they?" Sarah whispered to Ma.

"I think it's the folks who bought the Travers farm," Ma said. She shushed Sarah. "The meeting is beginning."

The Travers farm was only a mile down the road! Sarah looked one last time. All she could see of the girl was one side of the sunbonnet. "Oh, thank you, thank you for a girl. But, oh, please let her be my age," Sarah prayed. "Please, Lord."

When she turned back, she saw that twinkle in Brother Parks's eyes again. Her voice lifted joyfully as Pa's booming voice led the singing. She thought she would never be able to listen to the preaching. But when Brother Parks began speaking, she could not turn away.

When the service was over, Sarah looked for the girl. She was standing beside her mother. Granny Hazel was talking to them. Suddenly, Sarah hung back. What if the girl didn't like her?

"Come, Sarah," her mother said. "We must speak to our new neighbors."

Sarah found herself face to face with the new girl. She had big blue eyes. But she did not have black hair. It was as golden as summer corn. And when she saw Sarah, a big smile lit her face.

"Hi," she said, and Sarah knew her prayers had really been answered.

# Chapter Twelve
# Answered Prayer

All Sarah's fears disappeared. The two girls found a quiet seat inside the schoolhouse. The girl's name was Jenny. She was Sarah's age, but she had been born in May instead of June. She liked books and spelling and dolls. She liked climbing trees and riding and maple sugar.

Brother Parks stopped beside her. "Do you know that God answers prayer now, Sarah?"

"Oh, yes," Sarah said happily. "Yes!"

When the other girl looked puzzled, Sarah explained about her prayer request.

"All year?" Jenny asked. "You prayed all year?"

"And longer," Sarah said. "If you look around, you'll not see many girls. Oh, Mrs. Taylor's little baby is a girl! I almost forgot! Let's go see the babies!"

The two girls hurried off to inspect the two new babies. Mrs. Taylor let them hold little Annie for a while.

"We'll start praying for her right away," Sarah promised. "So she won't have to grow up without a girl to play with."

Mrs. Taylor laughed, but Sarah was not joking. She meant what she had said. She made Jenny promise to pray with her. "Just think," Sarah told her. "All those years I spent without a girlfriend."

Although school was out all during the spring planting, the girls had plenty of work to do. But their mothers agreed to release them for at least an hour a day. After doing their chores, the two girls met by the old covered bridge.

They played with their rag dolls. They climbed the biggest trees. They took off their stockings and risked a spring cold by wading in the icy water.

But most of all they talked. Sarah could not be with her new friend enough. She began to wish that school would start sooner.

Sometimes Sarah worked in the fields with her brothers. She liked the planting. The fields lay in lacy green circles of trees. The sun warmed them, but the spring wind kept them cool. She knew that the seeds she planted in hills or rows would make fine, strong plants.

While they worked, the boys teased her about Jenny.

"Now there'll be three in first grade," William said suddenly. "Where will you all sit?"

Sarah stopped, the seeds falling from her hand. There were only two seats at each desk. She and Jonathan were sharing a desk. Jenny would not be sitting with her!

"You can always get Jonathan moved," Thomas said. He watched Sarah's face.

"Oh, no," she said, putting her hand to her mouth. "I couldn't do that."

"Good," Thomas said. "I thought you had forgotten about Jonathan."

Sarah gave him a funny look. She didn't want to admit it, but she had. She had forgotten all about Jonathan.

Now she wasn't as eager to get back to school as she had been. She thought and thought. But nothing helped. At last she decided to let God take care of it.

On the first day back, Jenny was waiting at the bridge. She was riding a little mare.

"She's nice," Thomas said, patting the horse's smooth flank. "Real nice."

"She's gentle. Could Sarah ride with me?" Jenny asked.

"I reckon," Thomas replied. "It'd give Old Clancy a rest. Three's quite a load."

"Thanks, Tom," Sarah said happily. She slid off Clancy. Jenny helped her climb up behind her.

The two horses walked along side by side. Jenny was kind enough not to let the mare go fast. They reached the schoolyard together.

"I'll tie her out with Clancy," Thomas offered.

"Thank you," Jenny said.

She and Sarah slid down and left Thomas to take care of the horses. Sarah almost passed Jonathan. He was playing kickball with another boy.

"Hi, Sarah," he called. "You found another girl!"

Sarah blinked. "You grew!"

Jonathan grinned. "Ma had to make me new clothes."

"This is Jenny," Sarah said. "She moved into the farm below us. Jenny, this is my friend, Jonathan. And this is Matthew, one of the second graders."

Jenny said hello and gave Jonathan a big smile. "I'm in first grade," she said.

They were still talking when Mrs. Walker rang the bell. The children lined up and entered the classroom. Jenny waited in the back. Sarah and Jonathan went to their seats. Sarah saw an empty seat in the second-grade row. It was beside Matthew. She sighed. "That'll be Jenny's seat," she thought.

Jonathan didn't put his things up. He went to the front to speak to Mrs. Walker. She looked at Sarah and smiled.

"Jenny," she called. "There's a seat down here for you."

Jonathan waved at Sarah and slid into the seat beside Matthew. Right away he and Matthew were comparing slingshots. Sarah held her breath as Jenny walked down to sit beside

her. She squeezed her eyes shut. When she opened them, Jenny was there.

"It really happened," Sarah said to herself. "It really did. There's another girl on Yonder Mountain."